"HELLO READING books are a perfect introduction to reading. Brief sentences full of word repetition and full-color pictures stress visual clues to help a child take the first important steps toward reading. Mastering these story books will build children's reading confidence and give them the enthusiasm to stand on their own in the world of words."

—Bee Cullinan
Past President of the International Reading
Association, Professor in New York University's
Early Childhood and Elementary Education Program

"Readers aren't born, they're made. Desire is planted—planted by parents who work at it."

—Jim Trelease
author of *The Read Aloud Handbook*

"When I was a classroom reading teacher, I recognized the importance of good stories in making children understand that reading is more than just recognizing words. I saw that children who have ready access to story books get excited about reading. They also make noticeably greater gains in reading comprehension. The development of the HELLO READING stories grows out of this experience."

—Harriet Ziefert
M.A.T., New York University School of Education
Author, Language Arts Module,
Scholastic Early Childhood Program

PUFFIN BOOKS
Viking Penguin Inc., 40 West 23rd Street, New York, New York 10010, U.S.A.
Penguin Books Ltd, 27 Wrights Lane, London W8 5TZ (Publishing & Editorial) and
Harmondsworth, Middlesex, England (Distribution & Warehouse)
Penguin Books Australia Ltd., Ringwood, Victoria, Australia
Penguin Books Canada Limited, 2801 John St., Markham, Ontario, Canada L3R 1B4
Penguin Books (N.Z.) Ltd, 182–190 Wairau Road, Auckland 10, New Zealand

First published in Puffin Books, 1988 • Published simultaneously in Canada
Text copyright © Jane Fine, 1988
Illustrations copyright © Mary Morgan, 1988
All rights reserved • Printed in Singapore for Harriet Ziefert, Inc.

Library of Congress Cataloging-in-Publication Data
Fine, Jane.
Surprise! / Jane Fine; pictures by Mary Morgan.
p. cm—(Hello reading!)
Summary: A surprise is in store as three children prepare
breakfast in bed for their mother.
ISBN 0-14-050814-7
[1. Mothers—Fiction.]   I. Morgan, Mary, ill.   II. Title.   III. Series: Ziefert, Harriet.
Hello reading! (Puffin Books) ; 11.
PZ7.Z487Sv   1988   [E]—dc19   87-26216   CIP AC

# Surprise!

**Jane Fine**
**Pictures by Mary Morgan**

PUFFIN BOOKS

Everyone is sleeping
in this house.

It is time to wake up.

First Sam gets out of bed—
very quietly.

Next Meg gets out of bed—
very quietly.

And then Jo gets
out of bed.

# "Quiet, Jo!"

Sam and Meg and Jo
tiptoe down the stairs.

"Quiet, cat!" says Jo.

They all tiptoe
into the kitchen.

Sam gets a tray.

Meg gets a plate.
Jo gets a mug.

Juice on the tray.
Cookies on the tray.
Flowers on the tray.

Cat on the tray!

Get down, cat!

Sam and Meg and Jo
tiptoe up the stairs—
very quietly.

They put the
tray down—
very quietly.

Sam and Meg and Jo
tiptoe to their rooms.

Sam says, "I have mine."
Meg says, "I have mine!"
Jo says, "I have mine, too!"

Juice on the tray.
Cookies on the tray.
Flowers on the tray.

# Three presents
# on the tray!

Knock on the door.

"Time to wake up!"
yell Sam and Meg and Jo
very loudly.

Surprise!
Happy Birthday!